Jan Stewart is an academic, writer and cat lover.
She lives in Devon with her husband, Richard.

The Cats' Book
of Christmas Carols

Jan Stewart

Illustrated by Richard Stewart

AUSTIN MACAULEY PUBLISHERS™

LONDON * CAMBRIDGE * NEW YORK * SHARJAH

A CIP catalogue record for this title is available from the British Library.

ISBN 9781528947343 (Paperback)
ISBN 9781528972208 (ePub e-book)

www.austinmacauley.com

First Published (2020)
Austin Macauley Publishers Ltd
25 Canada Square
Canary Wharf
London
E14 5LQ

For Thani, Pyewacket and Monty,
who always joined in any singing and inspired this book.

With thanks to Richard Stewart who illustrated the book.The following felines freely offered to model: Crosby Stanton-Allen displaying his gold ribbon, Purdy James wading through snow and Zara Hamilton-Church climbing a Christmas tree. Further cat friends happily posed for pictures.
In addition, the following photographers kindly contributed copyright-free illustrations via Pixabay: *Arlouk* photographed the singing Siamese, *Adina Voicu* the smiling cat in the hat, *Phongwarit* the three oriental cats, *Uschi* the gift wrapper, liliy the silent meower, Kapa65 the hunting cat, *AllNikArt* the wise cat and *Alexas Fotos* the cat who didn't like his hat and disliked collars with bells even more.
Should any of the models' associates not have been mentioned, the author offers her apologies and will make full acknowledgements in
re-prints where possible.

Holly and Mistletoe

Don't sit under boughs of holly.
Fa la la la laa, la laa, laa, laa.

Prickles in your paws ain't jolly.
Fa la la la laa, la laa, laa, laa.

It's much nicer, as you know-oh.
Fa la la la laa, la laa, laa, laa.

To sit under mistletoe.
Fa la la la laa, la laa, laa, laa.

Frankincensed

Our cat Frankie got locked out
On the Feast of Stephen.
Snow fell right up to his snout,
Deep and crisp and even.

As he thawed out, Frank, incensed,
Wailed up from the flo-oor,
"Please install a large cat flap
In the kitchen do-o-or."

I Saw Three Cats

I saw three cats come creeping in
On Christmas Day, on Christmas Day.
I saw three cats come creeping in
On Christmas Day in the morning.

And what was in those cats all three
On Christmas Day, on Christmas Day.
And what was in those cats all three
On Christmas Day in the morning.

Some stolen salmon and turkey
On Christmas Day, on Christmas Day.
Some stolen salmon and turkey
On Christmas Day in the morning.

As all the bells on Earth do ring
On Christmas Day, on Christmas Day.
My meal's a half-chewed turkey wing
On Christmas Day in the morning.

Hunting in a Winter Wonderland

Robin sings.
We are list'nin'.
See his red
Feathers glist'nin'.
A beautiful sight,
For cats out at night,
Hunting in a winter wonderland.

Fast asleep
Are the blue birds.
And there seem
Very few birds
Out flying tonight,
Beneath the moonlight,
Hunting in a winter wonderland.

If we're unsuccessful, we'll have chicken.
And we'll lick our plates of every crumb.
But we would prefer a bit of livestock,
With the fur and feathers
Still stuck on.

So for now
We'll chase pheasant,
As they taste very pleasant.
And hide from the owl,
Who's out on the prowl,
Hunting in a winter wonderland.

Christmas Costs

While kittens hang their socks by night
For Santa Claus to fill,
Their parents worry at the cost
And how they'll pay the bill.

The Gift Wrapping Carol

Joy to all cats,
They're wrapping gifts,
And paper's just the thing
To crumple, crease and roll upon
And put prints of your soles upon
Whilst tangling bits of string,
Yes, tangling bits of string,
Whilst ta-a-a-angli-ing bits of string.

Joy to all cats,
They've sellotape,
And this you know is best
To remove all loose fur upon
And lick till all the sticky's gone,
Whilst unrolling the rest,
Yes, unrolling the rest,
Whilst u-u-unro-o-o-o-o-lling the rest.

Joy to all cats,
The gifts are wrapped,
So come and make a vow.
To find those that are our-our-ours,
Use all your sniffing powow-ers.
And open them right now,
Yes, open them right now,
We'll tear at and o-open our gifts right now.

Silent Meow

Silent meow,
Noiseless meow,
Roll around
Any old how.
Pat a le-e-eg wi-i-th your paw.
Rub your hea-e-ed o-on a jaw.
These are tricks all cats pla-ay
Whe-en they want their own way.

The Cats' Christmas Tree Carol

Away out of danger
All cats like to meet
To hold for their kittens
A traditional treat,
With great yowls of laughter
At the fun it can be
When a cat's left alone
With a decked Christmas tree.

"You can break several baubles
And fuse all the lights
And give to the fairy
A few friendly bites,
And swing from the tinsel
Before jumping free
To admire the effects
Of a wrecked Christmas tree".

White Whiskers

I'm dreaming of some white whiskers
Just like the ones I used to grow;
That I twitched and charmed with,
 And tickled arms with,
And flicked at snowflakes in the snow.

I'm dreaming of some white whiskers
As mine now don't look quite right
Since I got my nose up too tight
'Gainst the flaming Christmas pud last night.

The Alley Cats' Carol

Hark! All alley cats come sing
Feline praises to the king.
Peace on Earth is not allowed
Till we've caterwauled and yowled.
When the dawn comes, we will rest
Knowing we must do our best
To protect our ears from those
Humans who are so disposed
To attempt a loud and long
Rendering of Christmas song.

The Three Cats from Orient Carol

Christmas Eve

We three cats from Orient are
Nibbling toast and caviar
Canapes set out on trays.
Oops here comes a car...

Ooh, ooh...

Throw the dog a turkey drum.
Then when all the humans come,
He'll get blamed,
Chastised and shamed.
Lucky he is so dumb.

Christmas Day

We three cats from Orient steal
Remnants from the Christmas meal.
Chewing, licking, biting, nicking
Anything with appeal.

Ooh, ooh...

Bacon rolls, we like those best
With a slice of turkey breast.
Brandy sauce
For final course.
No-ow-ow we must rest, so-o...

Throw some food down on the floor;
Open up the kitchen door.
As dog comes in we'll go runnin'
And he'll get blamed some more.

Ooh, ooh...

Every dog must have his day.
At least that's what canines say.
But they learn
To their concern
Siamese rule, OK!

The Twelve Days of Christmas

On the first day of Christmas
I would like for tea
A partridge wrapped in pastry.

On the second day of Christmas
I would like for tea
Two tasty ducks and
A partridge wrapped in pastry.

On the third day of Christmas
I would like for tea
Three jugged hares,
Two tasty ducks and
A partridge wrapped in pastry.

On the fourth day of Christmas
I would like for tea
Four coq au vin,

Three jugged hares,
Two tasty ducks and
A partridge wrapped in pastry.

On the fifth day of Christmas
I would like for tea
Five chicken wings,
Four coq au vin,
Three jugged hares,
Two tasty ducks and
A partridge wrapped in pastry.

On the sixth day of Christmas
I would like for tea
Six geese a braising,
Five chicken wings,
Four coq au vin,
Three jugged hares,
Two tasty ducks and
A partridge wrapped in pastry.

On the seventh day of Christmas
I would like for tea
Seven salmon steaming,
Six geese a braising,
Five chicken wings,
Four coq au vin,

Three jugged hares,
Two tasty ducks and
A partridge wrapped in pastry.

On the eighth day of Christmas
I would like for tea
Eight meat loaves mincing,
Seven salmon steaming,
Six geese a braising,
Five chicken wings,
Four coq au vin,
Three jugged hares,
Two tasty ducks and
A partridge wrapped in pastry.

On the ninth day of Christmas
I would like for tea
Nine noisettes grilling,
Eight meat loaves mincing,
Seven salmon steaming,
Six geese a braising,
Five chicken wings,
Four coq au vin,
Three jugged hares,
Two tasty ducks and
A partridge wrapped in pastry.

On the tenth day of Christmas
I would like for tea
Ten turkeys basting,
Nine noisettes grilling,
Eight meat loaves mincing,
Seven salmon steaming,
Six geese a braising,
Five chicken wings,
Four coq au vin,
Three jugged hares,
Two tasty ducks and
A partridge wrapped in pastry.

On the eleventh day of Christmas
I would like for tea
Eleven pies a piping,
Ten turkeys basting,
Nine noisettes grilling,
Eight meat loaves mincing,
Seven salmon steaming,
Six geese a braising,
Five chicken wings,
Four coq au vin,
Three jugged hares,
Two tasty ducks and
A partridge wrapped in pastry.

On the twelfth day of Christmas
I would like for tea
Twelve roasts a roasting,
Eleven pies a piping,
Ten turkeys basting,
Nine noisettes grilling,
Eight meat loaves mincing,
Seven salmon steaming,
Six geese a braising,
Five chicken wings,
Four coq au vin,
Three jugged hares,
Two tasty ducks and

Cats' Advice to Humans

Never buy a little cat for Christmas.
Wait until its past.
Then you'll know if
Your interest in cats will last.

Please don't buy a little cat for Christmas.
It is not a toy,
There to entertain
Your little girl or boy.

It will live till your golden days
And will need food every day.
It might scratch all your furniture
And there'll be vets' bills to pay.

So don't buy a little cat for Christmas.
It's not right you know,
For cute kittens into great big cats must grow,
And many greet New Year
Abandoned in the snow.

Jingle Bells

ıgle bells, jingle bells, jingle all the way,
ıgle from our collars that arrived on Christmas Day.
1,
ıgle bells, jingle bells, jingle all the way,
ıgle round the garden warning birds
fly away.

her presents are
oright pink catnip mouse
ıat we love to toss and gnaw
ıd chase around the house.
t treats for our lunch,
rkey for our tea,
en we curl up nice and warm
ı any comfy knee.

ıng quietly)

,
gle bells, jingle bells, now they make no sound,
rn from off our collars and then
ried underground.

,
gle bells, jingle bells, every cat has found,
e is more exciting when those bells are not around.

The Senior Cat Carol

If your cat is getting old,
Keep it inside from the cold.

Brush it gently every day,
This will keep fur balls at bay.

And make sure it has a place
Where it can find peace and space.

CPSIA information can be obtained
at www.ICGtesting.com
Printed in the USA
BVHW022158181121
622019BV00022B/376

9 781528 947343